I0817601

THE DIGGER AND THE CHRISTMAS TREE

JOSEPH KUEFLER

HARPER
An Imprint of HarperCollins*Publishers*

It was Christmas Eve.
Digger and the crew were busy.

Lighting.

Hanging.

Decorating.

"It looks so merry," said Crane.
"Like a Christmas village," said Plow.

"The only thing left to decorate is the tree," said Hauler.

"Let's go," said Digger.

Plow cleared a path to the forest.
The big trucks followed.

"Decorating the Christmas tree is my favorite," said Dozer.

"Mine too," said Crane.

The tree stood tall.

“So much room for presents,” said Plow.
“Santa is going to love it,” said Hauler.

"Let's decorate," said Digger.

The other big trucks agreed.
So Hauler tipped his bucket.

But his bucket was empty.
"We are out of decorations," said Digger.

"No decorations means no Christmas tree," said Crane.
"No Christmas tree means no Santa," said Dozer.
"No Santa means no presents," said Plow.

The crew's Christmas was broken.
Digger did not know how to fix it.

Digger noticed a chipmunk scurrying by.

"Excuse me, furry friend," said Digger.
"Can you help us decorate our Christmas tree?"

Squeak squeak, said the chipmunk.

"Pine cones?" asked Plow.
"What for?" asked Crane.

"Will you show us?"
asked Digger.

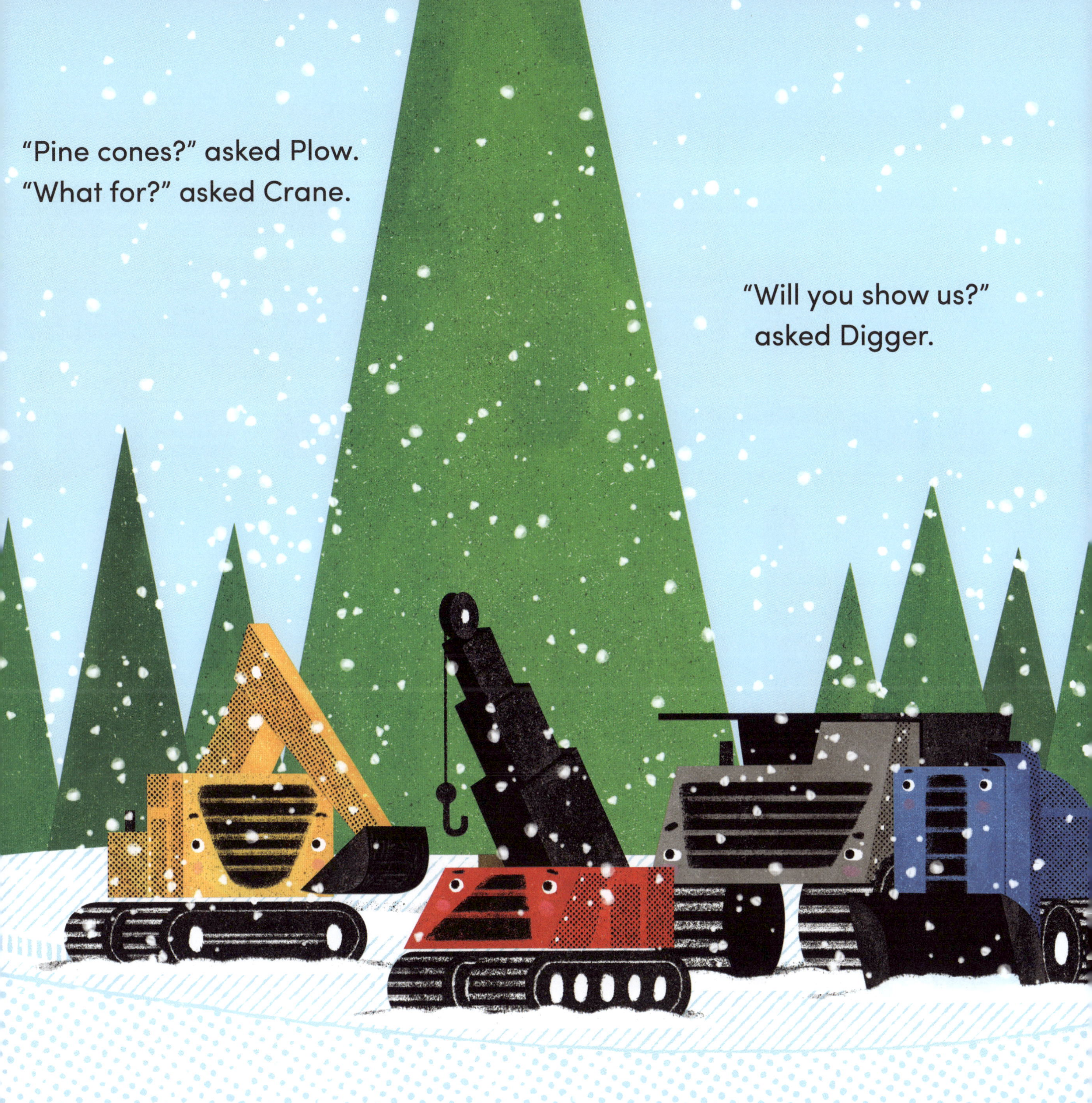

Together, they searched.

And strung.

And turned the pine cones into something special.

"How festive,"
said Crane.

"They're perfect,"
said Plow.

"Let's keep decorating,"
said Digger.

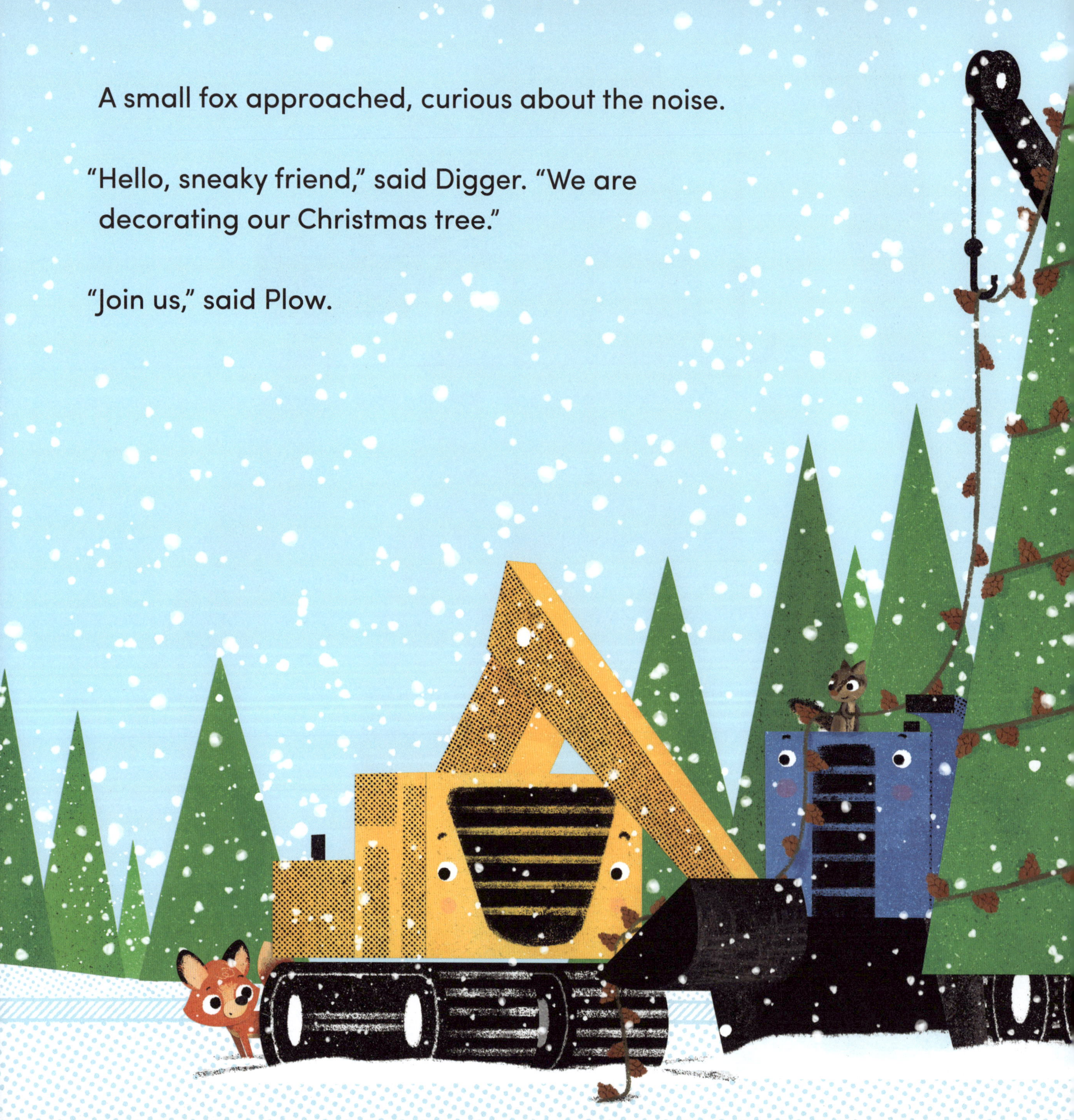

A small fox approached, curious about the noise.

"Hello, sneaky friend," said Digger. "We are decorating our Christmas tree."

"Join us," said Plow.

Bark bark, said the fox.

"Berries?" said Dozer.
"But why?" said Hauler.
"Let's find out," said Digger.

Together, they collected.
And snacked.

And turned
the berries into
something beautiful.

"How jolly,"
said Plow.

"I just love them,"
said Crane.

"What next?" said Dozer.

A cardinal appeared.

"Hello, flying friend," said Digger.
"Would you like to help too?"

Chirp chirp,
said the cardinal.

"Twigs?" asked Crane.
"Into what?" asked Plow.
"Will you teach us?" asked Digger.

Together, they gathered.
And grouped.

And turned the twigs
into a topper.

"The critters saved Christmas," said Digger.
The big trucks cheered.

“Now that’s a tree,” said Dozer.
“Santa will love it,” said Hauler.

"I hope Santa brings lots of gifts," said Plow.
"We made new friends," said Digger.
"Friends are the best gift of all."

The other big trucks agreed. So did the critters.

Their work was done.

The whole crew celebrated into the night.

Feasting.
Singing.

Waiting for Santa to come.

DIGGER'S
GUIDE TO MAKING
GARLAND

GATHER

Collect objects from nature or your home—ideally natural objects, like pine cones, spruce sprigs, and dehydrated orange slices. You will also need twine or string.

MEASURE

Determine how much string you need by measuring the space you plan to hang your garland. You can use a ruler, a tape measure, or your arms.

STRING

Place your objects on your string by tying them on or by using glue. If you are using hot glue, ask an adult for help. If any of your objects have holes, you can thread the string through.

SORT

Organize the objects into piles. Being organized will make the next step easier. The number of objects required depends on how long you would like your garland to be.

DESIGN

Create a pattern using the objects you have gathered. Try a few different patterns before deciding which you like best. Not into patterns? No problem! Order your objects at random.

TIE

Tie a loop on each end of your string to complete your craft. If you know how to tie your shoes, the same knot will do. If you cannot tie, ask someone for help.

HANG

Hang your garland somewhere special—on the fireplace mantel, your tree, your front door, anywhere. Or gift your garland to a friend or loved one.

To Erik,
for the gift of our friendship

HarperCollins Children's Books, a division of HarperCollins Publishers,
195 Broadway, New York, NY 10007

HarperCollins Publishers, Macken House,
39/40 Mayor Street Upper, Dublin 1, D01 C9W8, Ireland

The Digger and the Christmas Tree

harpercollinschildrens.com

Library of Congress Control Number: 2024949570
ISBN 978-0-06-342739-6

Typography by Joseph Kuefler and Dana Fritts
25 26 27 28 29 RTLO 10 9 8 7 6 5 4 3 2 1

First Edition